FAST COMPANY

WINNING SEASON

FAST COMPANY

RICH WALLACE

VIKING

VIKING

Published by Penguin Group

Penguin Young Readers Group, 345 Hudson Street, New York, New York 10014, U.S.A.

Penguin Group (Canada), 10 Alcorn Avenue, Toronto, Ontario, Canada M4V 3B2

(a division of Pearson Penguin Canada Inc.)

Penguin Books Ltd, 80 Strand, London WC2R 0RL, England

Penguin Ireland, 25 St Stephen's Green, Dublin 2, Ireland (a division of Penguin Books Ltd)

Penguin Group (Australia), 250 Camberwell Road, Camberwell, Victoria 3124, Australia

(a division of Pearson Australia Group Pty Ltd)

Penguin Books India Pvt Ltd, 11 Community Centre, Panchsheel Park, New Delhi - 110 017, India

Penguin Group (NZ), Cnr Airborne and Rosedale Roads, Albany, Auckland, New Zealand

(a division of Pearson New Zealand Ltd)

Penguin Books (South Africa) (Pty) Ltd, 24 Sturdee Avenue, Rosebank, Johannesburg 2196, South Africa

Penguin Books Ltd, Registered Offices: 80 Strand, London WC2R 0RL, England

First published in 2005 by Viking, a division of Penguin Young Readers Group

1 3 5 7 9 10 8 6 4 2

Text copyright © Rich Wallace, 2005

LIBRARY OF CONGRESS CATALOGING-IN-PUBLICATION DATA

Wallace, Rich.

Fast company / by Rich Wallace.

p. cm.

Summary: When sixth-grader Manny Ramos, one of the fastest runners on the youth football team, joins the new track club, he hopes that his light weight will be a benefit in racing against more experienced guys.

ISBN 0-670-05942-0 (hardcover)

[1. Running—Fiction. 2. Teamwork (Sports)—Fiction. 3. Competition (Psychology)—Fiction.

4. Size—Fiction.] I. Title.

PZ7.W15877Fas 2004

[Fic]—dc22

2004012480

Printed in U.S.A.

Book design by Jim Hoover

Set in Caslon 224 Book

For Garion, Cheyenne, and Ben

· CONTENTS ·

A New Opportunity

*M*anny and Anthony hauled their football equipment into the big storage area behind the middle school gym. The coaches were packing the stuff away after a successful season.

Assistant coach Lou Alvaro took Manny's helmet and said, "I've been waiting for you, Ramos. I'm starting a new program that's perfect for you." He handed Manny a photocopied sheet of paper:

HUDSON CITY CHARGERS
Youth Track and Field Club
Practice starts December I at the high school track.

—Indoor meets in winter
—Outdoor meets in spring and summer
—Road races year-round
Coach Lou Alvaro

"That sounds awesome," Manny said.

"Yeah," Anthony said, grabbing a corner of the paper and reading. "I'm definitely up for that."

"You could throw the shot put," Manny said.

Anthony frowned. "Yeah," he said slowly, "but I could run, too. I ain't that fast, but I lost twelve pounds during football season. If I drop a few more I'll be chasing you around."

Anthony Martin was the biggest kid in sixth grade and towered over Manny, who was barely five feet tall. He'd been a starting football lineman on both the offense and defense. Manny had mostly played on the kickoff squad.

"I love racing," Manny said. "Where are the indoor meets? Our gym is too small, isn't it?"

"Mostly in New York City," Coach Alvaro said. The young coach was tall and lanky. He worked with the receivers during football season. Some days he would run wind sprints with the team, and he always outran everybody.

"The New York Armory Track and Field Center has one of the best indoor tracks in the country," Coach said. "And they have a ton of meets. We'll compete there three or four times this winter, plus a few meets in Jersey City and at some of the colleges."

Manny had been one of the fastest kids on the football team. And when they ran long distances—like five laps around the field—he always finished ahead of everybody else.

"I'll probably run the mile," he said.

"That's what I figured," Coach Alvaro said. "And Anthony, you can run whatever event you want. I don't care how fast you are. I want people who are ready to work hard and have fun."

"That's me," Anthony said. He grabbed Manny under the arms and lifted him into the air. "Is there a Manny throw, Coach? I could toss this guy about fifty feet."

Coach laughed. "No, but Manny's right. You'd be a great shot putter. You can run, too."

Manny tried to wriggle free from Anthony's grip. "Can you put me down now?"

Anthony set Manny down and grinned broadly. His chubby brown cheeks seemed to glow. "We should start running today," Anthony said. "Want to go to the track?"

"Yeah," Manny said. "In about an hour. I gotta stop at home first."

"Me, too," Anthony said. "And I need something from my locker."

Manny carefully folded the paper into neat quarters and tucked it into his shirt pocket. The boys walked through the gym toward the school's sixth-grade wing.

"I am *so* psyched," Manny said. "I love to race. It's like pure effort, you know?"

"I can imagine," Anthony said. "Like sacking a quarterback or something."

They turned the corner in the hallway and Anthony stopped walking. "What's that?" he said, pointing to his locker.

A small piece of paper was taped to Anthony's locker. It said, ANTHONY: THE HAPPY HIPPO in red letters.

"That is so stupid," Manny said. He walked over and tore the paper from the locker. "What, are we in kindergarten?"

Anthony shook his head. "Jerks," he said softly. He opened his locker and took out his math book.

"So stupid," Manny said again.

"Forget it. I've been hearing crap like that since I was born."

"Yeah, but that's so pathetic," Manny said. "A sign on your locker?"

"You think they'd say it to my face?" Anthony raised his eyebrows and made a fist. "I don't think so."

"What babies."

"Forget it," Anthony said again, but Manny could tell that he was hurt.

"Let's get out of here," Manny said, and they headed for the exit.

On Track

Manny jogged all the way home. He could run all day. He'd been a scrub on the football team, but he knew he'd do well in track.

Five-year-old Sal was sitting at the kitchen table when Manny arrived home, drawing a picture of a truck. He was a smaller version of Manny, with dark, curly hair and deep brown eyes.

"Donald called you," Sal said. "Right after you left."

"Probably wanted to go drop off his football stuff with me."

"He said to call him."

"I will."

Donald had been Manny's closest friend for several years. Both had tried out for football for the first time this fall, and both had spent most of the time watching from the bench.

"Guess what, Sal?" Manny said. "There's gonna be a track team for kids. Isn't that great?"

"Yeah!"

Sal adored his older brother. "You're the fastest guy around, Manny," he said. "Can I be on the team, too?"

"Hmmm." Manny kneeled and looked his brother straight in the eyes. "You could run under the hurdles, maybe." He tickled Sal.

Sal laughed and broke away. "Really. I want to run."

"Tell you what. You can run with me sometimes. And in a few years, I'm sure you can get on the team."

"I'm really fast, Manny."

"I know it, buddy."

Manny dialed Donald's number and let it ring six times. Finally Donald answered.

"You turn in your stuff?" Manny asked.

"Yeah. Where were you?"

"I went earlier. I tried to call you."

"I slept late."

"You hear about the track team?" Manny asked.

"Yeah," Donald said flatly.

"You up for it?"

Donald snorted. "You kidding? Running is punishment, man."

"No," Manny said, drawing out the word. "It's beautiful."

"For you maybe," Donald said, laughing. "You've got bird bones or something. Or invisible wings. For the rest of us, it's torture."

"So you could do the long jump," Manny said. "Or the high jump."

"I'll think about it," Donald said. "But I doubt it. Anyway, you want to come over and watch TV or something?"

"Can't," Manny said. "I'm meeting Anthony at the track to work out."

"You guys are crazy. Work out for what?"

"Track. Practice starts in two weeks. We want to be ready."

"Whew. Gonna be cold all winter," Donald said. "I think I'll be hibernating."

"You'll miss out."

"I'll survive."

Anthony was standing on the track stretching when Manny arrived. Even though he'd lost weight, Anthony still had a heavy body. He was wearing a gray sweatsuit and a blue knit cap with an orange Mets logo on it.

"You warmed up?" Manny asked.

"Pretty much. You?"

"Yeah. I ran all the way over. What should we do?"

Anthony shrugged. "Sprint, I guess. I never ran track before. You're the expert, aren't you?"

"No way," Manny said. "But I think we should start out slow and build speed after a couple of laps. Let's try that."

"How far?" Anthony asked.

"The straightaway is 100 meters," Manny said. "Why don't we run the straights and walk the turns? I tried that a few times during the football season when I was mad about not playing."

"When I get mad, I eat," Anthony said. "We'll try it your way."

They walked along the first turn. Manny broke into a steady run as they reached the backstretch, and Anthony stayed with him. But it was obvious that Anthony was going nearly full speed just to stay with Manny. He was already puffing as they reached the beginning of the second turn.

"You all right?" Manny asked.

"Yep . . . no problem."

Manny smiled. The hard rubber track felt great under his feet. This was what he was meant to do. "Gorgeous day," he said.

Anthony just nodded.

They reached the front stretch and Manny ran a little faster. Anthony was running all-out now, but he kept up with Manny's pace. Manny felt as light as a feather.

"You're a speedy little rat," Anthony said as they slowed to a walk. He wiped his brow with a sleeve. "We doing another lap?"

"Definitely." Manny knew he could do at least ten more laps like that. "You can take a break after that. I'll probably keep going."

Anthony fell behind on the next sprint but caught up to Manny on the turn. "One more," Anthony said, breathing hard. "Let's make it a race."

"You're on." Manny had barely worked up a sweat.

They jogged the last ten yards to the straight-away, then broke into a sprint. Anthony was able to stay close to Manny for a few seconds but then fell behind. Manny raised his arms at the finish line, making two fists and shouting, "Victory!"

"Right behind you!" said Anthony. He bent over with his hands on his knees, struggling to catch his breath. "Whew," he said. "That cold air burns the throat."

"Felt good, though," Manny said.

Anthony nodded. "Good start. But that's enough for me."

"I'll keep going," Manny said. "I feel strong. I'll do two miles like that."

"I'll wait."

Manny was fully warmed up now and decided to

jog the turns instead of walking them. Anthony began walking around the track, and Manny caught up to him after running another lap.

"You need a drink?" Anthony asked.

"I will. When I finish."

"What do you want? I'll get us something."

"A Gatorade would be good. You need money?"

"Nah, I got it. I'll be back in ten minutes."

Manny finished the workout and bounded up the metal bleachers, stopping at the top to look down the hill. There was the Hudson River, with the New York City skyline on the other side looking close enough to touch on this clear November day. Somewhere over there was the Armory Track and Field Center. He'd never heard of it before today, but now it was foremost in his mind.

What would it be like, racing against kids from all over the metropolitan area? He didn't think there was anybody his age in Hudson City who could stay with him for a mile, but what about in Brooklyn or Queens or Hoboken? How good a runner was he?

Anthony had returned with the drinks, and

Manny walked down to the track. "Great work-out," he said. "You've got some speed, Anthony. This is going to be a great winter."

"I don't know," Anthony said. "You make it look so easy. What'd I run? 400 meters altogether. That ain't so good."

"We'll keep at it," Manny said. "I'm a distance runner. You can't expect to run as far as I do. Little by little, you'll get better."

Anthony nodded. "Yeah, I know. I'll be out here again tomorrow. I'll be ready when the season starts."

"Me, too," Manny said. "I can't wait. This team is going to be the best thing that ever happened to me."

Raisins

*D*onald came over that night and played poker with Manny and Sal and their parents at the kitchen table. The boys often played for nickels and dimes, but Manny's parents said they'd only play for raisins.

"What am I going to do with all those raisins I win?" Donald asked.

"Eat 'em," Manny said.

"Five-raisin limit," said Dad.

Donald rolled his eyes. "They aren't even my raisins," he said, taking a handful from the box.

"It's just for fun," Dad said, winking at Donald. "For the pure joy of the game."

Mom shuffled the cards and dealt the first hand. "Deuces wild," she said.

"Manny's gonna be in the Olympics," Sal said.

"That right?" said Dad.

Manny nodded. "One of the coaches is starting a track program. I already started working out."

"That's great," said Mom. "You too, Donald?"

Donald winced. "I don't know. Running isn't my idea of fun." He looked at his cards and changed their order. He pressed two fingers against his lips.

"Donald's more of a thinker," Manny said with a bit of sarcasm.

It was odd that Donald managed to stay as thin and wiry as Manny despite eating a ton and exercising as little as possible. He was a sharp contrast to Anthony, who worked out all the time but seemed to gain weight with every mouthful he ate.

"Track's a good sport for a small guy," Dad said. "Who else is on the team?"

"I don't know. We don't start practice for a couple of weeks. Anthony Martin's going to be in the sprints."

Donald set down his cards and stared at

Manny. "You're kidding, right?" he asked.

"No."

"What's he gonna do? Roll along the track?"

"Real funny." Manny turned to Sal. "Hold your cards so we can't see them," he said.

Little Sal brought his cards closer to his face and peered over them.

"Anthony works his butt off," Manny said. "He ran with me this afternoon."

"I could run circles around him," Donald said.

"Maybe, if you tried," Manny said. "Anthony's pretty quick. And at least he's out there doing it."

Donald chewed on his lip and nodded. "You got me there."

"You have two weeks to sign up," Manny said.

"I'll think about it." Donald looked at Manny's mom and pointed to the table. "Two," he said, sliding two cards toward the dealer.

"Can I run with you tomorrow, Manny?" Sal asked.

"Sure. You can jog over with me. Want to join us, Donald? One o'clock at the track."

Donald was frowning at the new cards he'd

picked up and playing with a couple of raisins. "We'll see," he said. He looked up and smiled. "I'll sleep on it tonight. You never know."

Manny and Sal jogged along Central Avenue on Saturday afternoon. As they approached the high school track, they could see Anthony walking toward them. He waved and started jogging, too.

Sal hugged Anthony's legs as they met and Anthony reached down and tickled him. "You gonna run with us, Sal?"

"Yeah. Manny said I could."

"You'll beat us by a mile," Anthony said. "How are we supposed to keep up with a little pony like you?"

"He'll take it easy on us, right Sal?" Manny said.

"No way. I'm *fast.*"

The afternoon was colder than the day before, but there was no wind at all. Sal was wearing big blue mittens and a shiny sweatsuit. Manny had black sweatpants and a long-sleeved red warm-up jersey from last year's soccer team.

"My legs are sore from yesterday," Anthony

said. "Haven't sprinted that far in a while. Probably *never.*"

"Well, most of the indoor sprint races are about sixty meters, I think. So you're already ahead of the game."

Anthony nodded and started jogging as they reached the track. "I'll take one easy lap to warm up," he said. "Then we can get started."

"Donald said he might show up," Sal said.

"Yeah, well let's not hold our breath waiting," Manny said. "I've got a feeling Donald is at home watching a football game on TV."

"Too bad for him," said Sal. "He's missing all the action right here."

Digging Deep

*T*wo weeks went by quickly. Manny and Anthony continued to work out most days, and other kids joined them a few times. But not Donald.

Twenty-six kids showed up for the first practice session. A few snowflakes were falling as Coach Alvaro greeted the athletes—sixteen boys and ten girls. Manny was glad to see Vinnie DiMarco and several others from the football team waiting in the bleachers.

"Welcome to the world's most exciting sport," Coach said, smacking his black mittens together.

"How many of you have been in a track-and-field program before?"

Three of the girls raised their hands. None of the boys.

"I started running for a club when I was about your age, and I've been at it ever since," Coach said. "There's nothing like racing to your potential, digging deep and giving everything you've got."

"What club?" asked one of the girls.

"The Shore Athletic Club," Coach said. "I'm still a member, almost twenty years later."

"You must be ancient," said the girl. Manny'd had a few classes with her—Sherry Allegretta. She always had a wisecrack to make. And she'd always ignored Manny.

"I'm older than the hills," Coach said with a smile, although he wasn't even thirty. "That's one great thing about track and field. There's something for every age. Kids, high school, college, and way beyond that."

"You ran in college?" Sherry asked.

"Yeah," Coach said. "Rowan University in South Jersey."

"Were you good?"

"Pretty good. All-American on a relay team. Now let's see what you guys can do. Take two laps easy. Then we'll stretch. Let's go."

"I'm a jumper, not a runner," Sherry said.

"Jumpers need to run, too."

Manny led the runners onto the track and began moving at a brisk pace. He was already warmed up from running over from home, and his excitement level was high.

Manny was several yards ahead of the next runners as he rounded the second turn. But as he ran along the front straightaway, he heard footsteps coming closer.

He glanced back and there was Sherry, gaining on him with every stride. *This isn't a race,* Manny told himself. *Let her show off during the warmup. Wait until we start training.*

Sherry came up alongside Manny on the backstretch, and he increased his pace a bit so she wouldn't pass. Sherry was about his height, with thick reddish hair that bounced on her shoulders as she ran. She was looking straight ahead, focused on the track.

As they rounded the final turn, Sherry began to sprint, pulling ahead of Manny as she moved into the second lane. Manny wasn't about to let that continue. He opened his stride and began a near-sprint, moving back into the lead and finishing slightly ahead.

"Whoa," Coach said as they slowed to a walk. "That was supposed to be a warm-up, guys. Save some of that fire for the workout."

"No problem," Manny said, but he was breathing rapidly. "I always sprint at the end of a warm-up."

Coach smiled. "I thought you weren't a runner, Sherry," he said.

"You never know," she replied. "You need speed on the long-jump runway. And maybe I'll do some racing."

"You look like a natural."

"I used to be a gymnast," she said. "Got tired of that."

Manny stared at Sherry. She glanced back with what seemed like a bit of an edge, but then looked away and began to stretch, reaching for her ankles and shutting her eyes. She was faster than most of the boys. And the back of her sweatshirt said GET USED TO THE VIEW.

The other runners were finishing now, with Anthony jogging in with the final group. Coach told everyone to spread out near the finish line, and he led them through a series of stretches.

"Today we'll all work out together," he said, "until we figure out the best events for everybody. In a few days we'll break into two groups—sprinters, jumpers, and throwers in one; middle- and long-distance runners in the other. But there'll be lots of overlap. Sprinters need endurance, and distance runners need speed."

"Will the girls run with the boys?" Sherry asked.

"Yes. In the meets, boys and girls will compete separately, but we'll all train together. Everybody has different strengths and weaknesses. You'll all gain by training with the others."

Manny kept his eyes on the coach, but he knew Sherry was looking at him. She seemed very competitive. He'd have to work his butt off to stay ahead of her. Losing to a girl would not be cool.

"Today we'll do 200-meter runs, with a 200-meter jog between," Coach said. "That's half the track, and it's a basic workout distance. We'll do four of them, gradually building speed so the last one is an all-out sprint."

He split the group in two, with Manny joining Sherry, Vinnie DiMarco, and some others in what was obviously the faster section. DiMarco had been the quarterback on the football team, and he had good speed.

"Fun, huh?" Manny said to Zero Rollison as they jogged toward the starting line.

"Should be," Zero said. Zero had been given his nickname way back in first grade, when the teacher made a list on the blackboard of kids who were fooling around in class and would have to stay in for recess for two days. M.R. for Manny, D.J. for Donald, Z.Ra. for Zach Raymond, and Z.Ro. for Zach Rollison. Even as first graders, the kids were quick to pick up on that. He'd been Zero ever since.

"Steady pace, now," Coach said as the runners

got ready. "The idea is to finish the workout as strong as you started." He blew his whistle and they took off.

Manny, Vinnie, and Sherry were tightly bunched as they came off the turn and onto the straightaway.

"Steady!" Coach yelled.

Manny stayed steady, but he made sure that he held the lead. His quick strides brought him down the track, pumping his arms and pulling ahead of the others as he glided through the finish.

"You've got great form, Manny," Coach said as the runners approached the starting line for the next one. "Sherry, try to relax your shoulders a bit. Vinnie, stop gritting your teeth."

Manny finished first in the next two intervals, but he was winded. No way would he let up now. The final 200-meter run would be an all-out race. Everybody would be gunning for that one.

DiMarco took off like lightning, and Sherry was right behind him. It was all Manny could do to stay ahead of Zero on the turn, but as they reached the straightaway, his endurance paid off. Zero fell behind, and Manny shifted into the second lane and drew even with Sherry. Now he drove into a full sprint, and that effort carried him ahead of her. DiMarco's lead was too much to overcome, but Manny was gaining. He crossed the finish line just inches behind.

DiMarco reached over and Manny smacked his hand. "Nice job," Manny said.

"You, too."

They turned and watched the second group of runners finish. Anthony was struggling, but he was ahead of two others. He snatched off his cap at the finish line and wiped his face with it. "That is a *long* way to sprint," he said to Manny.

"Good running, though," Manny said, falling into step with Anthony as they walked toward the pile of sweatshirts and stuff on the bottom row of the bleachers.

"Those workouts with you paid off," Anthony said, still puffing hard. "I never would have survived this a month ago."

Manny found his warm-up top and his gloves and picked them up. Sherry was leaning forward against the fence, stretching out her legs. Manny walked past her without catching her eye.

But Sherry surprised him by speaking. "Great running," she said.

Manny looked over, making sure it was him she was addressing. She raised her eyebrows slightly, waiting for a reply.

"Thanks," he said. "You're fast."

"We'll be pushing each other all winter," she said. "That can't be bad."

"Definitely," Manny said.

"I think I'll be racing after all," she said. "Like Coach said, running and jumping go together."

Manny nodded. "You definitely should be racing," he said. "I mean, I'm fast. And you pushed me all day."

Coach blew his whistle and called everybody over. "We've got some real talent here," he said. "I want two more easy laps from everybody— walk some of it if you have to. We'll meet again two days from now, and then again on Saturday. There's a relay meet in New York in two weeks. We should be ready to race by then."

Manny felt another surge of energy when Coach mentioned the meet. Before he knew it, they'd be racing for real! He took off running again, envisioning that relay meet. This time, no one else stayed close.

Monopoly

Manny's locker was right next to Donald's. He leaned against it and waited after school a few days later. Soon Donald came bounding down the hall, running into a fifth-grader and nearly knocking her over.

"What's up?" Manny asked.

"Nothing. Just was getting drilled by Mrs. Luciano after English," he said. "She said I was fooling around in class. Would I do that?"

"No way," Manny said, solemnly shaking his head. Then he laughed. "You're the perfect student."

"Teachers *love* me," Donald said. "I'm *always* polite and attentive."

"Yes, you are. You deserve a medal or something."

"At least," Donald said. "They should maybe rename the school after me." He shoved his books into his locker and put on his coat. "You coming over today?" he asked.

Manny hesitated. "I need to run first," he said.

"I thought there was no practice on Fridays."

"There isn't. But I want to do some extra work. We got a meet coming up."

"You never hang out anymore."

"That ain't true," Manny said. "I swear, I'll come over in an hour or so. I won't be long."

"Yeah, right," Donald said.

They walked over to Anthony's locker. Anthony was looking at a sheet of paper and frowning.

"What's that?" Donald asked.

Anthony shook his head. "More crap," he said. "Somebody stuck this on my locker."

Manny took the paper. In the same red lettering as before, someone had written TRACK EVENTS:

Manny and Sherie—high-speed make-out session. Demarco—sprints and hair-combing. Anthony—pie-eating contest.

"They didn't even spell the names right," Manny said.

"Who is this jerk?" Anthony said. "If I catch him, he's dog meat."

Donald bent the paper toward him to read it. "It *is* kind of funny, though." He looked at Anthony and took a step back. "No offense. Pretty good line about DiMarco." He turned to Manny. "Something going on with you and Sherry, hotshot?"

Manny rolled his eyes. "I barely know her," he said.

Anthony took the paper back and crunched it up. "Idiots," he said, looking at the ball of paper. He put it on the shelf of his locker, then slammed it shut. "Let 'em laugh," he said. "I got some running to do."

Manny ran for half an hour along the side streets of Hudson City, struggling a bit up the hills but enjoying the rhythm of the running. He ran past

the tightly packed houses with their small back-
yards and narrow driveways, along rutted side-
walks, or right in the street, alongside parked cars
and under the bare-branched maple trees. The air
was cold but dry.

He quickly changed clothes after the workout.

"Mom, I'm going over to Donald's for a little
while," he said, coming down the stairs into the
kitchen. Mom was a bank teller and had arranged
her schedule so she'd be home when Sal finished
kindergarten each day. She was just starting to
prepare dinner.

"We'll be eating at six," she said. "Your dad will
be home early tonight, so don't be more than an
hour."

"Okay," Manny said. "That isn't much time."

"Well," she said, "if you're going to work out
every day, that doesn't leave as much time for
hanging out with Donald."

"I guess."

Manny and Donald had been tight as brothers
for a long time, but this past football season had
changed things a bit. Manny still considered

Donald his best buddy, but Anthony had become a close friend, too. And Anthony was a dedicated athlete. He took sports as seriously as Manny did. That made a difference.

Manny winced as he remembered the line on the paper about him and Sherry. She was a serious athlete, too. But a girlfriend for Manny? No way.

Donald lived three blocks over on one side of a two-family duplex. He had the Monopoly board set up when Manny arrived.

"I've only got an hour," Manny said.

"No problem," Donald said. "You want a drink or something?"

"Yeah, I'm thirsty. I ran about three miles."

They settled into the game, and Manny slowly built an empire of purple, green, and orange properties. Donald owned a couple of railroads, but he was getting clobbered until he landed on Boardwalk and cobbled together enough money to buy it.

"You're mine now," Donald said, rubbing his hands together in glee. A few turns later he added a couple of houses.

Manny rolled the die and his mouth fell open. "Oh, man!" he said, moving his little metal car ahead seven spaces. Right on Boardwalk! "How much do I owe you?"

"Six hundred bucks," Donald said. "The comeback has begun!"

Just then the phone rang. Manny looked over at the clock. "That'll be my mom," he said. "I'm late."

Donald answered the phone. "Hello," he said into the receiver. "He's on his way."

"Call it a draw?" Manny said.

Donald frowned. "I guess. Just when I had you nailed, too."

"Later," Manny said as he hurried into his jacket and headed for the door. "Catch you tomorrow afternoon. I've got practice at ten."

Manny ran down Donald's hill and up his own. He was home in less than two minutes.

"Record time," said Dad, giving Manny a hug. "You're not even out of breath."

"I can run all day," Manny said. "Smells great in here. I'm hungry."

Sal was already seated at the table. "Me, too!" he said. "Let's go, Manny. I'm starving."

They all sat down and Dad said grace. Manny's family was Catholic, but he'd always attended public school. Mrs. Ramos's roots were Irish and Italian, but Dad's parents had come over from Cuba. The family went to church most Sundays, and Manny had played several seasons for the parish soccer team.

"Let's rent a movie tonight," Dad said. "Have a family night."

"Something scary!" Sal said.

"Sure," said Dad. "Something scary."

Manny reached over and put his hand on top of Sal's head. "You won't keep me up all night, will you?" he asked.

"Nah," Sal said. "I'm brave. Nothing scares me."

Manny laughed. "Wait till you get older. Life is plenty scary sometimes."

First Race

Manny's dad and several other parents did the driving as the team made its way into New York City for the first track and field meet. Manny sat in the front seat of the station wagon and tried to stay calm, but he could barely sit still.

He was scheduled to anchor the sprint medley relay. Zero would start with a 200-meter leg—one lap of the track. Then Calvin Tait would follow with another 200-meter run. Vinnie DiMarco would take the baton for 400 meters. Then Manny would finish the race with an 800-meter leg. Later, that same group would run the mile relay (actually, 1600 meters), with each one running 400 meters.

"This is going to be awesome," Manny said, turning in his seat to face Zero and Anthony. "I can't wait to get on that track."

"Won't be long now," Dad said. They were on the George Washington Bridge over the Hudson River, crossing into New York City. "The Armory is right up here on 168th Street."

Manny looked down at the river glistening in the moonlight. Then he unzipped his gym bag for the third time that evening, checking again to make sure he had his new racing shoes and his jersey. Coach Alvaro had handed out the jerseys the day before—red tank tops with HUDSON CITY CHARGERS in black lettering.

They parked in a giant, multi-level garage, and Coach Alvaro led the runners and their parents on the chilly walk along Fort Washington Avenue to the Armory.

"Wow!" said Manny as they entered the arena. It was the largest indoor space he'd ever been in—twenty times the size of the gym at his school. The six-lane 200-meter track was brick-red and the turns were sharply banked. On the infield was an eight-lane sprint straightaway, pole-vault and long-jump runways, and an area for the high jump. A huge American flag and a U.S. Olympic flag hung from the rafters high above the track, and swarms of kids were jogging on the track or stretching on the infield.

The Hudson City Chargers stood and looked around the arena. Manny's mouth was open and his eyes were wide. He felt tiny. Was he ready for this?

Calvin let out a low whistle. "This is *some* facility," he said.

"Guess we'll find out what we're made of," Manny said. "This is the real thing."

"I'll get us registered," Coach said. "You guys take a few laps before the meet begins. Get used to those banked turns."

Manny jogged next to Calvin and Zero. "Let's go a little faster on this turn," he said after a few laps of the track. They began striding harder, racing through the turn and onto the backstretch.

"Weird," Calvin said as they slowed to a jog. "Feels like one leg's longer than the other. Or like you're running uphill sideways."

"We'll be all right," Manny said. "It's dry in here, though." His throat felt tight from the short sprint. Racing indoors would certainly be different.

An announcement came to clear the track for the first event.

"You guys run in about thirty minutes," Coach Alvaro told them as they joined the others in the bleachers. "Stay loose."

Soon came the announcement they'd been waiting for. "First call, boys' eleven-twelve sprint medley. Report."

Manny shivered. Everyone in the arena would be watching him.

"Let's go, guys," Coach Alvaro said. He handed DiMarco an index card listing the team name and the four runners, with an estimated time of 4:35. "Hand this to the clerk. Remember—stick to the inside lanes. If you get forced outside on those steep turns, you'll wind up running a lot of extra yardage."

Manny took a deep breath and they made their way out of the bleachers to the floor.

About eighteen relay teams gathered near the starting line. DiMarco went over and handed in the card. Manny took a seat on the floor and watched as older runners sprinted by on the track. *Fast,* he thought. *And strong.* Runners, coaches, and other spectators in the bleachers above the track were cheering and pounding on the railing as the leaders neared the finish line.

DiMarco came back and kneeled next to his teammates. "We're in the second section," he said. "That's good, I guess. We can watch the first heat and get a feel for how it goes."

Manny nodded and shut his eyes and slowly let out his breath. His armpits were damp with nervous sweat. The runners around him waiting for the race looked serious. Determined. Their jerseys said things like PEGASUS TRACK CLUB, WASHINGTON HEIGHTS YMCA, ROCKAWAY ROADRUNNERS.

Nearby, four guys were jogging in a tight single-file line, making sharp handoffs with a baton. Their shirts said *Bronx A.C.* in yellow script against a black background that was slightly darker than their various skin tones.

"Those guys look *good*," DiMarco said.

"They in our race?" Calvin asked.

"Same race, different section," DiMarco replied. "The *fastest* section."

The Hudson City runners stood and watched as that fastest section began. The 200-meter runners seemed to fly along the track, and the 400-meter runners were smooth and strong. Manny kept his eyes on the anchor runner for the Bronx A.C., who waited calmly at the line for his teammate to hand off the baton.

The Bronx A.C. runner took the baton and followed the two leaders for a lap before passing them both on the backstretch. He led comfortably for another lap, then seemed to accelerate as the others began to tighten. His lead grew steadily from there.

Manny looked up at the runner standing next to him, a tall, thin athlete from the Synergistic Track Club. "He's fast," Manny said.

The guy nodded. "That's Kester Serrano. He's wicked quick."

Manny gulped and stretched his arms high above his head. They'd be on the track any second now.

"Second section," called an official. "Let's go."

Zero and the other leadoff runners took their places on the track. Zero was in lane four. The runners would stay in their lanes for the first lap. The second runners would cut for the inside.

Zero stumbled as the gun went off but quickly recovered and stormed down the backstretch and around the second turn. Calvin was waiting, but he took off too soon and they fouled up the exchange. Calvin had to come nearly to a complete stop to grab the baton, and Hudson City was suddenly in last place.

Manny stared at the runners, barely blinking. DiMarco was bouncing up and down, waiting for the next handoff.

Calvin moved up to fifth before handing off, and DiMarco rapidly gained on the runner ahead of him. He moved into fourth place on his second lap, about twenty yards behind the leader.

Manny took the stick and sprinted through the first turn, opening a gap ahead of the fifth-place runner. He glanced up at the runners ahead of him. *Can't do it all at once*, he thought. *Move up steadily, then go all-out on the last lap.*

Manny could hear his teammates yelling his name, but his focus was directly on the track and the runners in front. After one lap he began to relax. After two laps he could sense that he was gaining.

Two runners were still neck and neck at the front of the pack, but the third runner had begun to fade. Manny went into the second lane on the turn and moved ahead of him.

The bell sounded for the final lap, and the two leaders began to sprint. Manny accelerated, too, gaining slightly, but not enough. On the last turn the second-place runner finally broke, tightening up badly and losing contact with the leader. Manny was five yards behind, but he still felt smooth.

"Kick, Manny!" came the cry from DiMarco, and Manny responded by finding another gear. Racing down the middle of the straightaway, he caught his opponent and surged ahead, crossing the line in second place.

"Great job!" Coach said as they gathered in the bleachers a few minutes later. "You guys ran faster than half the teams in the first section. You'll probably get medals."

Coach took Manny aside. "You ran 2:22, Manny," he said. "That's terrific for a first race."

"What did that other guy run?" Manny asked. "In the first section."

"Serrano? He was about 2:18." Coach patted Manny's shoulder. "That's close," he said. "You get in a race with him and there's no telling how fast you'll go."

Manny's second race wouldn't be for a couple of hours at least. He watched as Anthony and the others raced. Sherry ran a strong 800-meter leg, too. And Manny, Zero, DiMarco, and Tait had the thrill of claiming medals for their performance in the sprint medley.

Eventually, Manny and his teammates went back to the track to warm up for the mile relay. He glanced often at Serrano as they stretched and jogged. Manny would be running the third leg in this race, with DiMarco on the anchor.

The official looked up from his clipboard and spoke in a commanding voice. "Boys' eleven-twelve mile relay, listen up. First section: Lane one, Suffolk Striders. Lane two, Bronx A.C. Lane three, Hudson City . . ."

"Wow!" said DiMarco. "First section."

"We deserve it," Manny said. "We medaled in the other race."

"Fast company," said Calvin. He made a fist and raised it. "Big time."

Zero and Calvin made a clean handoff this time, as all six runners came in within two meters of each other. On the infield, Manny ran in place for a few steps, then jumped straight into the air. The race was close. "Let's go Calvin!" he yelled.

Kester Serrano took off his sweatshirt and shook his arms. It was obvious that he was running the third leg. Same as Manny.

The second runners completed their first lap, and an official waved the next group onto the track. Manny and the other five crowded onto the starting line.

"Spread out!" hollered the official, and each runner moved about an inch. Serrano's elbow was leaning into Manny's back.

Here they came. Calvin was falling off the pace of the leaders, but he was ahead of the Bronx A.C. runner and one other. In the chaos of the exchange, Manny took the baton in fourth place, about two yards out of third and another two yards ahead of Serrano. *Nobody passes me,* he thought as he set out in a full sprint.

The baton, light as it was, provided a nice counterweight as Manny leaned into the first banked turn, focused on the bright blue jersey of the runner just ahead.

On the backstretch, he could hear Anthony and the others yelling his name. Manny's breathing was fierce. *Hug that inside lane*, he remembered.

One lap gone, and he could sense Serrano just off his shoulder. Manny ran harder.

Serrano went wide on the turn and pulled alongside Manny, his legs and arms churning. Manny moved out slightly, too. He had caught the runner in front of him, but he needed to get past before Serrano boxed him in.

Suddenly the three of them were running abreast. The runner in blue accelerated. Manny matched his pace, but his arms and legs were growing tighter. As they headed into the final turn, Serrano was forced to move into the third lane in an attempt to get past the other two runners. They came onto the homestretch inches apart.

Every step was an effort as Manny sprinted for the finish. He could see DiMarco waving his arms, and Manny grimaced as he extended the baton and his teammate grabbed it.

Manny collided with the runner in blue and they held each other up as they stumbled off the track. "Nice race," Manny whispered.

The other runner just patted Manny's shoulder, too tired to speak.

DiMarco managed to hold onto fourth place. Serrano's team had a speedy anchor who moved up to second.

Manny recovered quickly, but his throat was dry and scratchy. He walked over to the pile of clothes where he'd left his sweatsuit.

Serrano was sitting on the floor near Manny's stuff. He had his shoes off and was massaging his left foot. He wasn't much taller than Manny, but he had large hands and feet to grow into. His hair was extremely short, shaved almost to the nub.

Serrano nodded to Manny. "You guys from Jersey?" he asked. He had a soft but intense voice, and he kept his eyes right on Manny's.

"Yeah." Manny coughed. His throat was dry and sore.

"Never heard of the Hudson City Chargers."

"We're brand-new."

"I figured," Serrano said. "Otherwise I'd know about you. I check all the results online. Find out who my competition is."

"You ran awesome tonight."

Serrano shrugged. "I do okay."

"You ever run here before?"

"Like for three years," Serrano said. "I got a bit of a rep. People know me."

"You the Armory champion or something?"

Serrano smiled. "Got third in the 800 at the Metropolitan championships last winter. The top two guys moved up to thirteen-fourteen, so I guess I'm the favorite this year. But there's *lots* of fast people who come here. White guy Patrick Bertone from Brooklyn was right on my butt last year, and this Nigerian from Flushing, Oscar Kamalu. Maybe you?"

"Hope so," Manny said.

Serrano reached up his hand and Manny shook it. "Kester Serrano."

"I know. Manny Ramos."

"The Armory rocks," Serrano said. "This meet tonight is kind of low-key, but wait till you see the place in January, February. *Everybody* is here then. From all over the city; it's like the United Nations. Asian dudes. Brothers. You got Jamaicans. Dominicans. *Long Island* people. And everybody's fast."

"Can't wait."

"Yeah, we'll be seeing each other," Serrano said. He stood and reached into the pocket of his sweatshirt, pulling out a pair of thin-rimmed glasses. He blew on the frames, wiped them on his shirt, and put them on. "You think tonight was quick?" he said. "Just wait, Manuel. You ain't seen *nothing*."

Basketball

Manny slept in on Saturday. It had been after midnight when they returned from the meet. Sal hadn't budged when Manny entered their bedroom, but he was waiting when Manny woke up that morning.

"Did you win?" Sal asked excitedly.

"Take a look," Manny said, pointing to his dresser. His two medals were there, and Sal hopped off his bed and picked them up.

"Wow!" Sal said. "You smoked everybody?"

Manny grinned. "Not exactly. Those are for a fifth and a fourth. But that's not bad for our first meet."

"I wish I had been there."

"Next time you will. It was awesome, Sal. It felt like being a pro athlete. People from all over were competing. Fast runners, but I held my own."

"Cool."

"Wanna go to a basketball game?" Manny asked.

"Definitely!" Sal said. "The Knicks?"

Manny laughed. "No. At my school. I'm meeting Donald and Anthony in a half hour."

"Great! Let's get breakfast and get out of here."

The two brothers walked down the hill and met Donald at the corner of the Boulevard. Donald was waiting for them; usually he was the late one.

"Where you been?" Donald asked. "I got here ten minutes ago."

Manny shrugged. "Slept late. We were in New York until almost midnight."

"Oh yeah, the big track meet," Donald said. "You guys get slaughtered?"

"Not hardly," Manny said. "We kicked some butt."

"Big deal. Anybody can run."

"Don't knock it if you haven't tried it," Manny said.

"I still say running is punishment."

"I bet you'd like it."

"No way."

They walked in silence for a few minutes along the Boulevard's rutted sidewalk, past small restaurants and liquor stores and a florist. Sal followed a few steps behind. When they reached 14th Street, a block from the school, Manny stopped under the big digital clock that jutted out from the bank building.

"What are you doing?" Donald asked.

"I told Anthony we'd meet him here."

"What for?" Donald's voice was impatient.

"To go to the game."

"Hope it's not crowded," Donald said. "He'll need three seats."

Manny frowned, but he just looked at Donald for a moment instead of challenging him. Finally he said, "What's your problem?"

"What?"

"You're always busting on Anthony. But never

to his face. He's a good guy, but he'd pound you if he heard that."

Donald waved his hand. "He'd never catch me."

"Don't be too sure."

Sal pointed toward the next corner. "Here he comes!"

Donald held up his hand for a high five as Anthony approached. "What's happening, bro?" he said.

Anthony smacked Donald's hand. "My man," he said. "How's it going?"

"It's going awesome."

Manny gave Anthony a gentle punch on the arm. Then he looked at Donald curiously. *What a fraud*, he thought. *Acting all buddy-buddy with Anthony two seconds after ripping on him.*

The basketball team was playing against Lincoln. Hudson City was supposed to have a good team this year, but they'd gotten pounded in their opener a few days before. The wooden bleachers in the small gym were about a third full of spectators.

"There's Sherry," Anthony said, nudging Manny's arm.

"Yeah," Manny said. "She's here to watch Fiorelli. She's drooling over him."

Jason Fiorelli was one of the stars of the basketball team, just as he'd been in football. He was a carefree kid with good looks and great athletic skills. Manny liked him. He wasn't arrogant like a lot of the better athletes.

"Wish we had *him* on the track team," Anthony said.

"He told me he might join the team in the spring," Manny said. "After basketball."

"He'd make a good sprinter," Anthony said. "Probably a good jumper, too. Or a hurdler."

"Or just about anything," Manny said.

Donald sighed. "Can we talk about something besides track? It's *boring*."

"Not to us," Anthony said.

"To everybody else it is," Donald said.

Anthony looked around and smiled. "Everybody who? It's just us sitting here. You bored, Sal?"

"No," Sal said.

"See?" Anthony turned back to Donald. "Sal isn't bored."

Donald frowned. He leaned back on the bleachers and watched the basketball game.

At halftime, Sherry climbed the six steps of bleachers and walked over to the boys. She was wearing her Chargers track shirt over a black turtleneck, and she had her hair pulled back in a ponytail.

"You guys recovered from last night?" she asked.

"Pretty much," Manny answered. "You running later?"

"Yeah. Just two miles easy on the track. You?"

"Same thing."

"Might as well do it together," Sherry said.

"Okay."

"I'll meet you about half an hour after the game, okay?"

"At the track?"

"Yeah."

Donald grabbed Manny's arm. "Wait a minute," he said. "I thought you were coming to my house after the game."

"This is important," Manny said. "I'll come over later."

Donald shook his head. "You act like it's the world championships or something."

"Maybe to me it is."

Donald rolled his eyes. Sherry sat in the row ahead of them, facing the boys instead of the basketball court. She and Manny and Anthony talked about the track meet for most of the second half. Donald didn't say a thing.

Manny arrived at Donald's house after supper, fresh from a run on the track. "You and your girlfriend get good and sweaty?" Donald asked.

Manny felt his face get warm with embarrassment. "We were just running," he said as he followed Donald up the stairs to his room. "Get a grip. It isn't like that."

"I thought you couldn't stand her."

"She's okay. I mean, she's not exactly what I'd call sweet, but she's a good athlete. She's not so bad if you get to know her."

"Seems like you're getting to know her real well."

"We just *jogged*," Manny said, getting annoyed. "Drop it, all right?"

"Okay, hotshot."

"What does it matter to you, anyway?"

"It matters because you've always got something else to do these days," Donald said sharply. "We used to hang out every day, but now it's like, 'No, I got a track meet.' 'No, I gotta jog with Sherry.' 'No, I gotta work out with fat-boy Anthony.'"

Donald took a seat at his desk. Manny stared at him for a few seconds. "You could have joined the team," he said.

"I don't *want* to join the team. Get it? I don't want to run."

"All right," Manny said. "But I do. What's so bad about that?"

"Nothing, as long as you remember who your friends are. Me."

"You're my friends?"

"I'm your *best* friend."

"Yeah." Manny let out his breath and scratched his head. He started to speak, then stopped.

"What?" Donald said.

"Yeah, you're my best friend," Manny said. "But you seem to have a problem with me having other friends. What's that about?"

Donald gave Manny a hard look. "We used to hang out every day," he said. "Now you've always got something else to do."

"True," Manny said softly. They'd been inseparable for the past few years, spending every afternoon at one of their houses or playing basketball at a playground or just hanging out on the Boulevard. But Manny had found something that really excited him, that allowed him to excel as an athlete. Donald wanted nothing to do with it. So what was Manny supposed to do?

The boys were quiet for a minute or so. Donald drummed his fingers on his desk. "So, you want to watch TV?" he asked. "Or play a game?"

"Let's see what's on TV," Manny said. "Maybe make some popcorn or something."

"Sounds good," Donald said. And they walked down the stairs to the kitchen.

"One question," Manny asked. "Why did you put those notes on Anthony's locker?"

"Who said I did?"

"Who else would have done it?"

Donald looked up at the ceiling with a grimace

on his face. "Just having fun," he said. "Too bad if he can't take it."

"He can take it," Manny said. "But it's stupid. Knock it off, or I'll tell him."

Donald shrugged. "Who cares?"

"I do. I don't like people making fun of my friends."

"Your friends," Donald said with a sneer. "I'm the best friend you ever had. Remember that."

"I never said you weren't. What I'm saying is, I've got other friends, too. Get used to it. Things change."

Tough Competition

*T*he guy seated next to Manny on the basketball court inside the track had his eyes shut,
nodding slowly to the rhythm of the music from
his headphones. His shirt said NORTH JERSEY STRID-
ERS. Other runners were pacing the floor or
stretching, all looking intense.

The gymnasium at Fairleigh Dickinson
University wasn't quite as large as the Armory, but
Manny was even more nervous for this meet. This
wasn't a relay meet; there were no teammates to
help carry the load. In a few minutes, Manny
would be out there for the 800-meter race with
nine opponents.

He checked his racing shoes—double-knotted with the laces tucked in—massaged his thigh, and took a deep breath. He knew nothing about the other racers, didn't recognize any of them from the meet at the Armory. This was primarily a New Jersey event.

"Boys' eleven-twelve 800. Step up."

Manny got to his feet and bounced in place a couple of times. He was warm and loose. They'd had time to jog a full mile before the meet, and he'd been stretching ever since. The track was the same length as the Armory's—200 meters—but the turns were flat.

He stepped to the starting line. The runners on both sides of him were tall and leggy. Manny crossed himself and shut his eyes.

"Take your marks," said the official.

Manny leaned slightly forward and exhaled hard.

"Set."

He clenched his fists lightly and stared at the track.

The gun fired and Manny surged from the line, darting to the head of the pack to avoid the jostling as runners fought for position. Coaches and teammates were shouting, but Manny's focus was entirely on the track. He could hear the padding of nine pairs of feet just behind him.

Pace yourself, he told himself. *Hold the lead, but be smart about it. Long way to go.*

Manny's goal was 2:18, the time Serrano had run at the Armory the week before. Who knew what Serrano would do this week; he was probably racing at the Armory again. All the results of the Armory meets were posted on the Internet, so Manny could compare his progress with Serrano's and everybody else's.

"33," came the call as Manny finished the first lap, still holding the lead. He needed to average under 35 seconds per lap to meet his goal for today. He felt strong.

Manny glanced behind him as he raced along the backstretch. Coach had told him never to do that, but he couldn't resist. Two runners were just off Manny's shoulder, but the rest of the field had fallen a few yards behind. These two seemed content to let Manny lead the way.

Each stride felt smooth, but Manny could feel his shoulders beginning to tighten. He passed through the end of the second lap at 67 seconds.

Fast, he thought. *Got to keep this up.*

Coach had told him that the third lap was often the most important one in a four-lap race. The runners were getting tired from a quick start and were saving some energy for a finishing kick. A strong runner could put away the race with a solid third lap. But the temptation was to hold back a little.

Manny surged into the turn, testing his opponents to see if they'd stay with him. They did more than that. The North Jersey Strider runner went wide on the turn and moved into the lead.

Don't let him get away, Manny thought. *Stick with him.*

They pounded down the backstretch in a tight cluster, but the leader surged again coming off the second turn. Manny opened up his stride on the straightaway, pulling away from the third-place runner and turning it into a two-man race.

"1:43," came the cry as the bell sounded for the final lap. Manny quickly did the math; that lap had taken 36 seconds. They were slowing down. *So what!* Manny hollered inside his head. *It's a race! Forget about the time.*

Manny moved to the outside edge of the first lane and stuck within inches of the leader. Around the turn and into the backstretch, his aim was to stay with this guy.

Arms pumping furiously, they headed into the final turn, puffing and grunting as they began an all-out sprint. The leader moved out to the line between the first and second lanes, forcing Manny to go even wider if he wanted to get past.

Onto the straightaway, just fifty meters from the finish. Manny dug for everything he had left. Closer, closer, and suddenly he had the lead. Leaning forward with no air in his lungs, his throat burning and his arms feeling like cement. The finish line, the tape against his chest. He won it!

Manny got off the track and settled to his knees. He put his fingertips to his pounding forehead and shut his eyes, gasping for breath. He lowered his hands to the floor and crouched like that for a few seconds, waiting for his head to clear and his breathing to slow down to normal.

Suddenly he felt hands around his waist and was pulled gently to his feet. "Fantastic race," said Coach Alvaro. "Walk it off, buddy. Don't lie there in a heap."

Manny took a few slow steps and inhaled deeply. He looked up at the coach and gave a pained smile. "Caught that sucker," he said softly.

"You sure did," Coach said. "You're a tough little guy, Manny. There's no quit in you."

Manny looked up at the bleachers toward his teammates and family. He raised his fist when he locked eyes with his father, then turned to the coach.

"What was the time?" he asked.

"2:19. Pretty darned good." Coach smiled. "Serrano better watch out, huh?"

Manny gave a tight smile and nodded. He'd used every ounce of strength and speed he had in him. Where would he find even more?

A Higher Level

Manny and Sal got up early Monday morning to have breakfast with their dad before he left for work. Dad drove a truck for a package delivery company and was out of the house before seven every morning. Often he didn't return until seven at night.

"Will you make us French toast, Daddy?" Sal asked, rushing into the kitchen in his pajamas.

Dad was seated at the kitchen table, drinking a cup of coffee and reading *The New York Times*. He glanced at the clock. "Sure," he said. "We'll have to hurry. Get out the bread, Sal."

Manny took a frying pan out of the cupboard. He turned on the burner and poured oil into the pan.

"I want six pieces!" Sal said. "I'm starving."

"Let's start with three apiece," Dad said, rubbing Sal's hair. "We can always make more."

Sal took a seat and tapped his knife and fork on the table. "Can I bring your gold medal for show-and-tell, Manny?" he asked.

Manny nodded. "Yeah. You promise to take good care of it, though. Who knows if I'll ever win another one."

"I'm sure you will," Dad said. "I think you've found your sport."

Sal got up and opened the refrigerator. He took out the carton of orange juice. "You working late tonight, Daddy?" he asked.

"You never know," Dad said. "Been real busy lately."

Just then Mom walked into the kitchen. "We're a busy family," she said. "I've got three active boys here, don't I?"

"Active and hungry!" Sal said. "You want French toast, Mommy?"

"I sure do. You guys are some team, making this feast so early in the morning. It smelled so good I got up before my alarm."

Manny set a plate on the table and motioned for his parents to sit down. "You guys eat first," he said. "Me and Sal will take the second batch."

"Great," Dad said. "I've got just enough time to eat and get out of here."

"Not us," said Sal. "We got an hour. Will you watch cartoons with me after we eat, Manny?"

"No problem," Manny said. "I hope Bugs Bunny is on."

Manny ran an easy three miles after school. He was feeling good about his performance in Sunday's meet. He'd made an all-out effort and had nothing left at the end, but Coach assured him that he'd get faster with more training and a bit more racing experience.

Running under 2:20 in just his second 800-meter race was a great indication of Manny's potential. A guy like Serrano, for example, had three years of racing under his belt. Manny was still a novice, but he knew he'd be ready for the championship race in February.

After dinner, Manny sat down at the computer and found the Armory Web site. He clicked on *Results*. A listing of various meets, mostly high school and college, came up on the screen. He found the youth development meet from the previous Saturday and scrolled through, looking for the results of the eleven-twelve boys' 800.

There it was. Serrano had won the race, but he must have had quite a battle:

1. **Kester Serrano**   **2:15.8**
2. **Ryan Wu**   **2:15.9**
3. **Oscar Kamalu**   **2:16.2**
4. **Mario Torres**   **2:17.4**
5. **Lyndon Duncan**   **2:19.9**

Manny stared at the screen. *Four* guys had run faster than he had, and there were five others at 2:22 or better. Serrano was right; there were a lot of quick runners around.

Manny had felt like a big deal winning that New

Jersey race. Clearly, the guys across the river were running at a higher level.

Manny shut off the computer and climbed the stairs to his room. He checked the schedule Coach Alvaro had given him. They'd be running at the Armory again in two weeks.

Against Serrano and the rest of them.

Froot Loops

*T*he team trained hard for the next two weeks. Coach Alvaro had Manny concentrate on building his endurance, alternating distance runs with sessions on the track.

"I think you can run with anybody in the region," Coach told him. "Sure, they've run faster times than you have, but we'll see what happens when you go head-to-head."

That chance arrived quickly. Manny found himself in the 800-meters at a Saturday morning development meet at the Armory. More than fifty runners were signed up for the event. Manny was among the eight told to report for the top-seeded section.

Kester Serrano looked up at Manny from his seat on the floor, stretching out his legs. "Hey," he said softly, nodding.

Manny let out his breath. "Hey."

"Tough field," Serrano said.

"Yeah. That Wu?" Manny asked, jutting his chin toward a tall Asian kid warming up nearby.

"Yep." Serrano pointed toward some other runners. "Bertone and Kamalu. The boys are all here, Manuel."

A roundish official with short dark hair and a microphone said, "Let's go, gentlemen. On the track."

Manny had drawn lane two, sandwiched between Wu and Bertone. He knew he'd have to get out quickly. Everybody in the race had put up fast times already this winter.

"Runners set!"

Manny leaned forward. He was the shortest one out there.

The gun went off and the runners darted from

the line. Manny tried to squeeze ahead of Bertone, but the bigger runner extended his arm and pushed his elbow into Manny's ribs. It didn't hurt and Manny kept his balance, but he was forced to stay in the second lane as they rounded the first turn.

Manny dropped back slightly on the back-stretch and made his way to the inside lane. All eight runners were fast, and they were moving as a unit. The first lap went by in 33 seconds, with Manny running third behind Bertone and a runner in a yellow jersey.

Serrano came cruising by midway through the second lap, looking very smooth and in control. Manny was already feeling the pace, struggling just slightly.

They passed the midpoint in 66. Manny's goal in this race was 2:16, but the competition was more important than the time. He needed to show himself that he could take these guys.

The third lap hurt like crazy, but Manny stuck with the leaders. Bertone continued to set the pace, with Serrano second and Kamalu now third.

"1:41," came the call as Manny finished his third lap, just a yard or so behind the leaders. He was well ahead of his previous race, but his breathing was a struggle and his arms felt like lead. The three runners ahead of him accelerated toward the finish. It felt like the race would never end. Manny was fading badly.

Wu raced past him on the final turn, and then another runner swept by. Manny pumped his arms harder, but he had nothing left to give. He could hear the others coming up behind him, but he managed to hold them off and finish sixth.

Manny stepped off the track onto the infield. He held his arms across his stomach and walked stiffly toward the high-jump mat, where he fell face-forward and shut his eyes in agony. He'd never felt worse in his life.

"You all right?" came a familiar voice.

Manny sat up and rubbed his eyes. Sherry was standing next to the mat.

"I'll be okay," Manny said. "You run yet?"

"Soon," she said. "There's about a million heats in the boys' race. Nice job, by the way."

Manny frowned and shook his head. "I got toasted."

"Don't worry about it. You hung in there."

"I sucked."

"No you didn't."

Manny stood up and swallowed. "I gotta go," he said in a hurry, not sure what was going to happen next. All he knew was that he needed to get to a bathroom.

"Wish me luck," Sherry said as Manny hurried away.

"Luck," he said, not turning back. He waited for a pack of runners to pass by on the track, then quickly made his way toward the exit. The restrooms were on the next level. Manny hustled down the stairs, his spiked shoes making *click-click* sounds on the steps.

He barely made it to the bathroom in time, bending over the first sink in the row and vomiting up his breakfast in three quick heaves. Froot Loops, orange juice, everything. He turned on the faucet to rinse the sink, and leaned against the porcelain with his eyes shut.

After a minute he began to recover, and he cupped his hands to take water into his mouth. He rinsed and spit, then wiped his mouth with his arm. Two younger kids were staring at him.

Manny laughed gently. He felt much better already. The dizziness was gone and his stomach was relaxed. "Tough race," he said to the younger boys.

Manny took off his spikes and walked up the stairs barefoot. Serrano was on his way down.

"You win?" Manny asked.

"Barely," Serrano said. "Where were you?"

"Way back. No kick today."

"A fast pace like that takes it out of you," Serrano said. "We were all tying up. I barely got past Bertone at the finish."

"I just puked my guts out," Manny said.

"Comes with the territory," Serrano said. "You got e-mail?"

"What? Sure."

"Write down your address for me. I'll be in touch."

"Okay. Catch me upstairs."

"You got it."

Manny took a seat in the bleachers with his teammates, sipping from a bottle of blue Gatorade. His throat burned from the racing and the vomiting.

Coach came over eventually and took the seat next to Manny.

"How bad was my time?" Manny asked.

"Just over 2:22," Coach said.

"That's terrible. I'm supposed to be getting *faster.*"

"You were on pace for a 2:16 until that monkey jumped on your back," Coach said. "Listen, every good runner has races like that. It's just part of the learning curve. You stayed with those guys for most of the race. The tough guys keep at it, whatever they're up against. There's nobody tougher than you."

Manny nodded. He'd blown this opportunity, but there were plenty more ahead. He knew he could run faster. But those other guys—Bertone, Kamalu, Serrano—they were on a whole different level from him.

Two Meals Behind

*B*y the time they got back to Hudson City late Saturday afternoon, Manny was starving. He hadn't eaten since breakfast, and he hadn't digested anything all day.

Manny had ridden over with Calvin, Zero, and Anthony in Mr. Martin's van. As the runners unloaded outside the school, Manny had an idea. "Let's all meet for wings or pizza or something."

"Or both," Anthony said. "Villa Roma?"

"Yeah. Let's tell the others."

Many of the runners agreed to meet at 6:30 at the restaurant. Manny had enough time to walk home, shower, and call Donald.

And brush my teeth, he thought. His mouth tasted stale and pukey.

"How'd you do?" Dad asked as Manny entered the house. Sal and his parents were having dinner.

"Not good," Manny said. "Went out too fast and fell apart."

"Those are the breaks."

"Yeah. Okay if I go to Villa Roma? A bunch of people from the team are going."

"Sure," Mom said. "Didn't you get anything to eat at the meet?"

"No. I threw up after my race. I couldn't even think about eating until a little while ago. Now I'm starving."

"Do you want some pasta?" Mom asked. "Or Pepto-Bismol?"

"Nah, I'm all right. I just need a shower. We got any mouthwash?"

Villa Roma was right in the middle of town, and it attracted a young crowd. Most went there for the pizza and the video games. Manny looked through a stack of freshly washed T-shirts on his dresser, then thought twice and chose a blue button-down shirt from his closet instead.

Donald had said he'd show up later, so Manny walked downtown alone. The side streets were dark and cold, but the Boulevard was busy with traffic. Most of the restaurants were bustling.

Several of the runners were already at a big table toward the back when Manny arrived. He waved to Zero and Calvin.

Sherry and two other girls were there. She pointed to the seat next to her. "Sit here," she said.

Manny shrugged and sat down between DiMarco and Sherry. She was wearing jeans and a white T-shirt with TEEN QUEEN written on it in small, glittery beads. Her red hair was down. She smelled like perfume, but not too strong.

"Anybody order yet?" Manny asked.

"Just pitchers of soda," Sherry said. "We were waiting for you and Anthony to show."

"There he is." Anthony was walking over with a big grin. He had his medal pinned to his sweatshirt—third place in the shot put.

A teenage waitress came over and looked

around the table. "Big crowd," she said. "What's the occasion?"

"Anthony won a medal," said Zero, pointing across the table.

"So did Sherry," Anthony said. She'd placed fifth in the girls' 800.

"We're the fastest people in town," Zero said. "And the hungriest."

Manny asked for a hamburger, fries, a strawberry milk shake, and an order of wings.

"Feeling better, huh?" Sherry said.

"Feeling *empty*," Manny replied. "I'm two meals behind, at least." He patted his stomach. "Lots of room for expansion."

Sherry laughed. "You missed my race."

"Sorry. I was sick as a dog."

"Yeah. You turned white."

Manny shrugged. "I *am* half white."

"I mean you were *pale*. Like you were going to pass out."

"I know what you meant."

Zero pounded his fist lightly on the table and raised a glass of Coke. "A toast to Manny, who did the fastest running of the day," he said with a big grin. "*After* his race. From the track to the bathroom!"

Manny blushed and laughed. Anthony threw a wadded-up napkin at him. Then he opened his mouth wide and said, *"Raaaaalph."*

Sherry rolled her eyes. "Are you guys gonna be gross?"

"Who, us?" said Zero. "No way."

"Just make sure there's a clear path between Manny and the bathroom," Anthony said. "Don't get in his way, Sherry."

Manny shook his head with an embarrassed smile. He tapped his chest with his finger. "Guts," he said.

"We know," said Zero. "All over the sink."

"Very funny."

When the food arrived, Manny drank half of his milk shake before starting on the hamburger. By the time he'd finished the fries, he was full. "You want any of these wings?" he said to Sherry.

"Maybe one," she said.

"Anybody want these wings?" Manny said, louder.

"Send 'em over," Anthony said. "Me and Zero will polish them off."

Manny felt a smack on his shoulder. He turned to see Jason Fiorelli standing there, alongside Donald. "Not so fast with those wings," he said. "Save some for us."

"Where'd you come from?" Manny said.

"Donald called me. Told me you guys were hanging out here," Fiorelli said, reaching for a wing.

Manny looked over at Donald. They hadn't seen much of each other over the past couple of weeks. Was Donald hanging out with Fiorelli now?

Jason Fiorelli was considered the coolest kid in the sixth grade—an athlete and a comedian with good looks and the kind of attitude that never took anything quite too seriously. He was a star in football and basketball, and generally had at least a couple of girls following him around. He was fast and agile. The type of athlete Manny wanted to be. Sort of like Kester Serrano.

"Hi, Sherry," Fiorelli said.

"Hey," Sherry said flatly, looking past Fiorelli toward something at the front of the restaurant.

Donald brought a chair over from another

table and slid in between DiMarco and Manny.

"What's up?" Manny said.

"Nothing much," Donald replied. He tipped his head slightly in Sherry's direction and gave Manny a questioning look, like, *What's the story with you and her?*

Manny turned up his hand and gave an *I don't know* look back. Sherry had obviously been after Fiorelli this year. Jason hadn't caved, though. Maybe Sherry had given up the chase.

Manny caught Donald's eye and gave the same unspoken gesture about Fiorelli. Donald shrugged. "We been hanging out some," he said.

Sherry had gotten up and walked to the juke-box. She was leaning against it, looking at the selections. Villa Roma was known for having a good jukebox, although there was almost nothing current on it. Mostly classic rock and dance, plus a dozen or so Frank Sinatra songs and some big band stuff.

Manny left his seat and walked over.

"I've got a couple of quarters," he said when he reached Sherry.

"I already put in a buck." She pointed to the listing for "I Will Survive" by Gloria Gaynor. "What do you think of that?"

"Disco," he said dismissively.

"The *best* disco song of all time," she said. "What do you want, Aerosmith or something?"

"My dad plays the Doors every time we come in here."

"Okay." Sherry punched in the numbers for "Light My Fire." "That's for your dad. What about you?"

Manny studied the selections. He glanced back at the table. Nobody was watching them. Anthony was sitting with his chair tipped back, talking to Mary Pineda. Zero and Calvin were playing table football with a wad of paper.

"A New Jersey boy," he said. "State pride."

"Sinatra?"

"No. Springsteen."

"You got it," she said. "And one more for me." She chose Madonna's "Borderline."

Manny started to walk back to the table.

"Wait," she said.

"What?" He stepped over.

Sherry leaned with her back on the jukebox and wiped her hands on her jeans. "Nothing," she said.

"Come on. What?"

"I couldn't believe it when Jason walked in here."

"Why not?"

She looked over at the table. Jason and Donald were eating the wings and talking with their mouths full. She started to speak, then stopped.

Manny stood there flat-footed. He felt a trickle of sweat run down his side from his armpit.

"I asked him out about two weeks ago," she said. "To come *here* for pizza, believe it or not."

"So, what happened?"

"He said he'd get back to me. And he didn't."

"Oh."

"He acted like it never happened. The next day in school he said hello like he always does, then he walked away real fast. The day after that he started avoiding me."

Manny scratched his jaw. "Well," he said, "Jason gets a lot of attention from girls."

"No kidding," she said. "He could have just said *no.*"

"Yeah."

"I mean, it's not a secret that I asked him. All my girlfriends knew. So I ended up looking like an idiot."

Manny nodded. "Sorry," he said.

She shrugged. "It has its advantages," she said. "Made me run my butt off every day to stop thinking about it."

"Yeah. I can relate to that."

"How?"

"Not . . . you know. Not because of girls or anything. Just when I get frustrated. I run it out of me."

"It seems to work. I got over it." She tapped on the jukebox glass. "Then he came in here tonight." She shook her head. "Can I ask you something?"

"Sure."

Sherry glanced around the restaurant, then took a deep breath. "Can we go outside?"

"Sure." They got their coats and stepped out to the sidewalk. "What's going on?" Manny asked.

"Had to get out of there," Sherry said. She hesitated, then asked, "Do you think I'm too tough?"

"What do you mean? You have to be tough to be a runner."

She tilted her head back and squinted from the glow of the streetlight. "Too tough for a girl, I mean."

He looked at her for a moment. "Why should that matter?"

"I don't know. Somebody like Jason . . . I mean, what do guys think about a girl who . . . you know what I mean. I can beat most of the guys on the team."

"So?"

"Am I *girly* enough? I've been this tomboy all my life. And then I try to change my image a little, and Jason doesn't even respond."

Manny leaned against the building. Who was he to give advice to a girl? But he'd try.

"There's plenty of female athletes," he said. "There's nothing wrong with that."

"Yeah, but even for the other girls on the team, it seems like more of a social event than a sport," she said. "I mean, I want to kick *butt* when I'm racing. One reason I quit gymnastics was because I was *too* intense. I kept screwing up because I was trying too hard."

"You *gotta* work hard at sports. That's what I love about it."

"But does it turn guys off if a girl is like that?" Sherry asked. "My mind-set is a lot more like you and DiMarco than it is like Mary or the others."

Manny looked uptown at the digital clock by the bank. It was 8:18 and twenty-eight degrees. He buttoned the top two buttons of his coat and blew on his fist. "I don't know," he said. "All I know is when I'm in a race or a game or even in practice, I go all-out. I don't care what anybody thinks."

"Guys are supposed to be like that."

"I suppose."

"You're right, though. I need to be who I am." A few flakes of snow had started to fall. They appeared in the circle of light closest to the street-light then disappeared. "Thanks," she said. "You're all right."

"You, too."

Sherry gently swung her arm until her fist smacked Manny's shoulder. "Pow," she said. She stuck out her tongue, then smiled, turned, and went back into the restaurant.

Manny exhaled, and his breath came out in a stream of vapor. He looked back up the Boulevard.

His legs were tired. He'd sleep like a rock tonight. Rest tomorrow.

And on Monday he'd get back to work.

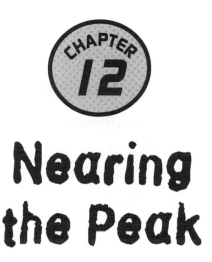

Nearing the Peak

On Monday, Coach Alvaro had Manny work on holding a steady pace, putting him through eight repeats of 200 meters at 33 seconds each with a 200-meter jog between.

On Tuesday, Manny ran four miles through the streets of town, concentrating on staying relaxed, especially going up the hills.

Wednesday's workout featured longer intervals: a set of four 400-meter trials with DiMarco, Calvin, and Zero.

And on Friday after school, the team headed for the Jersey City Armory for a low-key development meet. Coach had Manny run the mile for a change of pace, and he triumphed at the longer distance by steadily pulling away from the field.

"Good one," Coach said after Manny had recovered. "You've got one more shot at the 800 next weekend; then the Metropolitan championship is a week after that. I think you can win it, Manny."

"We'll see."

Manny was still haunted by his collapse in the last 800-meter race, and he was eager to erase the memory. He'd badly wanted to compete at that distance today, but Coach was firm in his belief that a mile would serve him better.

"Your speed is great; it's the endurance that you need to build," Coach said. "Be patient. You're just starting to peak. We'll get one more fast race in next weekend, then set you loose at the championship."

Manny walked over to Donald's late Saturday morning. A light snow had fallen overnight, but it was already beginning to melt. The winter had been mostly dry—a big plus for the track team, since they trained entirely outside.

Today Manny didn't want to think about training or racing. He needed a break.

Two days off, he decided. *Nothing but relaxing and eating.*

"What's going on?" Donald said when he answered the door.

"You up for hanging out?" Manny said.

"Definitely."

"You eat yet?"

"A little." Donald ran his hand through his hair. It looked like he'd just gotten out of bed. "I could eat again."

"Let's get some pizza."

"Sure. Then you want to go to the high school wrestling match?"

"Why not?" Manny had never been to one.

"I been to the last two matches," Donald said. "It's awesome."

They got pizza at Luigi's, a small place just off the Boulevard. "Better food here than Villa Roma," Donald said.

"Not as much fun, though," Manny said. Luigi's

didn't have a jukebox or video games. Just four tables set tightly in the front of the room. Most of their business was take-outs and deliveries.

Donald crammed the last of his second piece of pizza into his mouth. "Take that with you," he said, pointing to what was left of Manny's second piece. "I don't want to miss the first match."

"What difference does it make?"

"Hudson City's best wrestler is the smallest," Donald said. "Hector Mateo at 103 pounds. He's undefeated. Pins everybody."

They hustled along the Boulevard to the high school and got into the gym just as Mateo was taking the mat against a wrestler from Bayonne. Both wrestlers were lean and not very tall. But Mateo had thick muscles and was quicker than his opponent. He shot in low and gained control.

"I saw him pin a guy in sixteen seconds last week," Donald said.

The Bayonne wrestler managed to escape, but Mateo rapidly took him down again. This time, there was no escape. Mateo executed the pin in little more than a minute.

"The great thing about this sport is that you wrestle people your own size," Donald said. "Not like football, where we had to tackle guys who outweighed us by sixty pounds."

Manny nodded. His father had been a successful amateur boxer, and he had told Manny the same thing about that sport. He'd had his nose broken a couple of times, though.

"We could start wrestling when we get to seventh grade. You think you might?" Donald asked.

"I don't know. I never thought about it."

"You'd be good."

"Maybe. You?"

"I think so," Donald said. "I think I'd like it."

"Yeah, it would suit you." Manny pictured Donald out there, straining with all his might against another wrestler. "Hard work."

"I can handle it."

"Working out can be fun, believe it or not."

"Yeah," Donald said. "If you find the sport you like."

"That's the key."

Bayonne was strong in the middle weight

classes and wound up winning the match. Donald kept his eyes on the mat all afternoon. "Wrestling's definitely the sport for me," he said when it was over.

"That's great," Manny said. The wrestlers reminded him of runners, totally focused on the event, giving everything they had. And having to do it alone. No teammates could help you in a race or a match. Could Donald handle it? Why not? "You'd be a natural," Manny said.

"Probably. I got no body fat, and I'm strong for my size. Like you."

"Yeah. I don't think I'll be wrestling, though. I found my sport."

Relax and Push

Manny sat in the bleachers at the Armory the following Saturday and stared up at the giant American flag hanging from the rafters. Zero and DiMarco were warming up for the 400-meter race, but Manny could barely watch. He was more than nervous this time. He was scared.

This meet was called the New York Road Runners Invitational. Everybody was using it as a tune-up for next week's Metropolitan Championships. The bleachers were packed with athletes from New York City, New Jersey, and Long Island.

Manny had scanned the crowd and found most

of his biggest rivals. Serrano was stretching with his teammates down behind the high-jump mat. Ryan Wu was seated in the bleachers directly across the track. Oscar Kamalu was in a corner of the arena, sitting against the wall with his eyes shut and headphones on.

He hadn't spotted Patrick Bertone, but he did recognize several other quick runners. If he was ever going to run a fast 800, today would be the day. He needed that boost of confidence.

When the call came for the eleven-twelve 800-meter races, Manny and Sherry got out of their seats and headed down to the floor.

"Boys first again?" Sherry asked as they walked down the stairs.

"I think so," Manny said.

Sherry gave him a mischievous smile. "Hope you survive to see me run this time."

"Count on it," he said. He was in no mood for joking.

The roundish official stood near the side of the track with his clipboard. "Listen up, people," he said. "First section, boys' 800. Let me know you're here when I call your name. Lane one: Oscar Kamalu."

Kamalu stood up and said, "Here." Kamalu was muscular for a twelve year old. He filled out his purple jersey.

"Line up against the wall as I call you," the official said. He was wearing a white USA TRACK AND FIELD cap. "Ryan Wu?" he said.

Wu nodded from his seat on the floor, but the official didn't see him. "Ryan Wu?" he said again.

"Right here," Wu said. He looked deadly serious.

"When I call your name, let me know that you heard it. And smile, Ryan. It's only a race."

Wu shrugged and gave an embarrassed grin. He stepped over to stand next to Kamalu.

"In lane three, the famous Kester Serrano," said the official. "Then Manny Ramos. Daniel Singh. Elliott Carballo . . . Carballo?"

There was no response.

"Last chance, Carballo. There you are. Were you sleeping? Let's move."

When the eight runners had gathered, Manny

took a look around. He'd beaten a couple of these guys before, and he knew he could stick with the others if he ran a perfect race.

"No sign of Bertone," Serrano whispered to Manny. "He knows we're thinking about him. Wants to let us wear each other down this week, then surprise us in the championships."

"The big psyche job, huh?"

"Whatever. Good luck."

"You, too."

They lined up on the track and Manny shut his eyes, goading himself to hang in there, no matter how much it hurt. When the gun went off, he took the lead, making his way to the inside lane.

Relax and push, he thought as he pounded down the backstretch. He had no intention of leading for long, but he wanted to make sure he didn't get boxed in toward the back.

Manny eased the pace as he headed into the second turn, and Ryan Wu moved past him. So Manny was second as they finished the first lap in 34 seconds. That was only a little slower than he'd run the last time, but it made a big difference. He felt much stronger.

Manny held that position through most of the second lap, but Kamalu raced forward and took the lead as they reached the midpoint in 68 seconds. The runners were tightly bunched. The buzz from the bleachers grew louder.

Manny was tempted to glance back and check out the others as he rounded the turn. Instead, he kept his eyes on the leaders. Besides, he knew who was sitting just off his shoulder. Serrano. The only one who could be breathing that easily at this pace.

Nearly everyone in the Armory was standing and yelling now as the leaders moved toward the end of the third lap. Kamalu held the lead, with Wu right on his shoulder. Manny and Serrano were less than a stride behind. The others had begun to fall back.

The bell sounded and Serrano sprinted past Manny. The pain was nothing compared to last time; Manny still felt strong. It was a matter of speed now. He wasn't going to die.

Down the backstretch, Manny stayed with the leaders. Coming off the final turn, Kamalu, Serrano, and Wu were fanned out over the first three lanes of the track, with Manny inches behind. He was tying up, but so were the others. He dug deep, churning his arms. Serrano and Kamalu pulled away, but Manny nearly caught Wu at the finish.

He stepped off the track and bent over with his hands on his knees, gasping for air. He shut his eyes again and felt the warmth spreading over his face and ears. What an effort. He felt all right. He opened his eyes and stood tall.

Serrano was next to him, shaking his head and frowning. Oscar Kamalu had his arms raised toward a section of the bleachers where his team-mates were standing and applauding.

"Better this week than next, I suppose," Serrano said. "If you're going to lose, don't lose the big one."

The runners turned toward the giant score-board at the far end of the Armory, where the times of the leaders were already being posted.

1—2:14.7
2—2:14.8
3—2:16.1
4—2:16.2

Kamalu had run the fastest time of the winter, but Manny's 2:16 was also impressive. He shook his fist and said, "Yeah." He could go another second or two faster. He'd definitely be in contention at the championships.

By the time Sherry raced ten minutes later, Manny had recovered. He found a spot along the backstretch and kneeled at the side of the track, yelling for his teammate each time she ran past.

Sherry's hard work was paying off, too. Like Manny, she stayed near the leaders for most of the race. But she didn't quite have the finishing speed of the others and wound up fifth.

Manny hustled across the track, scooted around the high-jump mat, and picked up Sherry's T-shirt. He caught up to her and handed her the shirt. She kept walking and wiped her face with it.

"My legs feel like spaghetti," she said. She dropped to her knees. "I'm dizzy."

"It goes away," Manny said, gripping her arm. "You should keep moving."

"Okay," she said, getting to her feet. "Stay with me."

"No problem."

They walked a slow lap between the track and the outside wall, with Sherry's spiked shoes clicking on the wooden floor.

"You ran a good race," she said after a few minutes.

"You, too." Manny hesitated for a few seconds before adding, "Very tough."

Sherry raised her eyebrows. "That's me," she said. "Toughest girl in New Jersey."

"You are who you are," Manny said. "Don't compromise because of what others think."

"I know."

They reached the shot-put area, back behind the far turn. Anthony and a group of other competitors were waiting for the older throwers to finish. Anthony was slumped against the wall, staring into space. He gave a tiny nod of recognition as Manny and Sherry came over.

"You ready?" Manny asked.

"Very ready," Anthony said. "This is the worst part, waiting to get started."

"Yeah," Manny said. The anxiety before a competition was brutal. You got so keyed up, so worried that you'd fail. Then the event began, and it was such a release just to be out there competing. "Hang in there, Anthony. Stay focused."

Anthony nodded again and looked at his hands. Even good-natured Anthony was obviously feeling some tension.

Sherry put her hand on Manny's back and applied some pressure. "Gotta keep walking," she said. "Do the job, Anthony. We'll come back and watch you throw."

They walked a few more yards and Sherry whispered, "He needs to be by himself. No distractions. You know how it is."

"Definitely," Manny said. "There's some things you've just got to face by yourself."

"We'll catch up with him after he throws. He'll be a whole different person once it's over."

Instant Message

*I*n practice that week, Manny could feel his endurance building, could tell that he'd be ready to run faster than ever at Sunday's championship meet. He ran well ahead of the other Hudson City runners during long intervals, and even managed to outrun Zero and DiMarco and the other speedsters during the sprints.

Late Thursday afternoon he returned from a jog and sat down at the computer in the family room.

"You want to play a video game?" Sal asked, rushing down the stairs.

"Sure, Sal. In a little while. I just want to check out some basketball scores. See how Seton Hall did last night."

Sal stood next to Manny as he pulled up a newspaper Web site. "You gonna win on Sunday?" Sal asked.

"I don't know," Manny said. "I want to. I think I can. But there are some big-time runners in the race."

"Bigger than you?"

Manny shrugged. "So far anyway. But I'm feeling like maybe it's my turn now."

"I'll be yelling my head off for you," Sal said.

Manny gripped the back of Sal's neck gently. "I'll hear you."

A bulletin flashed on the screen: *kesterrano has sent you an instant message. Do you wish to accept?*

Kester Serrano? Manny thought. He must be thinking about the race, too.

Manny clicked on the *Yes* box. The conversation went like this:

kesterrano: Whazzup?

Mannyman: hey

K: Bertone went 2:13 the other night

M: No way. where?

K: Pratt Institute

M: FAST time

K: no kidding. slow track too.

M: OUCH

K: he be ready

M: sounds like it

K: me be ready too

M: yu, me, he be ready

K: yu, me, he, wu, kamalu. we ALL be ready

M: All of us

K: See you Sunday!

M: Can't wait.

The competition would be incredibly fierce. Manny turned off the computer and climbed the stairs to his room. He lay back on his bed and stared at the ceiling, preparing a strategy. If he could just stick with those guys until the final lap, there was no telling what might happen. Serrano, Kamalu, and Bertone had all run two or three seconds faster than Manny had this winter, and Ryan Wu was also a factor. He'd just have to gut it out, make sure they didn't open a gap, then kick like crazy.

It sure would be exciting. He almost wished he could be with Sal and their parents, watching the race from the bleachers.

CHAPTER
15

The Metropolitan Championships

*T*he day was cold and clear as Manny and his teammates walked along Fort Washington Avenue past the towering buildings of Columbia-Presbyterian Medical Center. Athletes of all ages and sizes were funneling toward the Armory Track and Field Center, dressed in colorful warm-up suits and talking excitedly.

Manny was quiet as they walked along. He had just one thing on his mind. The race.

Only a handful of Hudson City Chargers had qualified for this championship meet—Anthony in the shot put, Manny and Sherry in the 800, Zero and DiMarco in the 400, Calvin Tait in the 200, and Mary Pineda in the dash.

Sal kept pace with Manny as they neared the
Armory, wearing his own warm-up suit and carry-
ing a stopwatch. He looked hopefully at his brother a few times, but Manny was all business today.

"I find out who I am today, Sal," Manny said as
they entered the arena.

He'd have a long wait. The 800 was one of the
last events, so it would be hours before he'd run.
Plenty of time to get ready.

Lunch was a turkey sandwich with tomato and
mustard. His mom sat behind him in the bleachers and handed it to him, insisting that he eat.
"You've got to have energy," she said. "Your race is
still a couple of hours away."

"Okay," Manny said. He wasn't hungry, but he
knew she was right.

DiMarco was about to finish his section of the
400 meters. Zero had been fourth in an earlier
heat, and it didn't look as if DiMarco would do any
better. He was fifth as he entered the final straightaway, grimacing and driving as he tried to pick off

the fourth-place runner. He didn't quite get him.

"Tough competition," Mom said.

"Yeah," Manny said with a mouthful of sandwich. "Everybody in my race is quick as heck. Anybody could win it."

"Including you," Mom said.

"Including me."

Manny walked down the stairs to the bathrooms about forty-five minutes before his race. He'd seen most of his rivals warming up already—Oscar Kamalu going through some yoga-like stretches over in a corner, Ryan Wu jogging laps around the perimeter of the arena, Patrick Bertone putting in bursts of speed on the infield.

He saw Serrano in the hallway on the lower level, pacing back and forth, eyes fixed straight ahead. When Serrano saw Manny, he pushed his headphones off his ears and gave a hint of a smile.

"Ready?" Serrano asked, shaking Manny's hand.

"I am."

"I think we all are."

"Gonna be fast."

"Gonna be *brutal,*" Serrano said. "Championship meets aren't always fast, though. There's usually more strategy in the first two or three laps. Could take a big-time kick to win it, like a 30-second last lap or something insane like that."

"That *would* be insane," Manny said.

"Could happen," Serrano said. "Look at the field. You know what the winning time in this meet was last year? 2:16. There's four guys in the race who already ran faster than that this season. And everybody else is close."

Manny nodded. He suddenly felt even more nervous than before, partly because he could tell that Serrano *wasn't.* Confidence was sure to play a big part in the outcome. Whoever wanted it most would win it. Whoever had enough confidence to take a chance.

"Runners take your marks!"

Manny leaned forward and glanced at the ceiling, high above the track. To his left was Kamalu, whose forearm jutted firmly into Manny's. To his right was Serrano, taking a deep inhalation.

"Set."

Manny clenched his fists lightly. He held his breath.

The gun fired, and there was pushing and grunting as the eight runners bolted from the line. Bertone came cutting in from the outermost lane, streaking toward the front of the pack as they reached the end of the first turn. Manny was fourth, with Serrano on his shoulder.

Bertone's early charge gave him the lead, but he slowed the pace as soon as he'd established himself as the front-runner. All eight runners stayed in contact through the first lap and into the second, stringing out to nearly single file, but all within steps of the leader.

Bertone continued to lead as they rounded the second turn of the second lap. Manny could hear his name among the shouts of the spectators. He felt strong—almost too strong. The pace was slow.

Manny remained fourth as they neared the midpoint, following Bertone, Kamalu, and Wu. When he heard the time—69 seconds, he felt a surge of energy but also a flash of dread. At a pace like that, it would surely come down to an all-out sprint, and that would play right into the hands of Serrano, Kamalu, and Bertone. All had more pure speed than Manny did. If he was going to win this thing, he'd have to steal it now.

Third laps are where the toughest guys succeed. Coach had told him that many times this season. Manny was about to find out if it was true. He surged into the turn, moving out to the second lane and flying past Wu and Kamalu. On the backstretch he pulled even with Bertone, then kept going. By the middle of the next turn he was back in lane one, opening up a stride on the field, then two.

"Come on, Manny! Come on!"

Manny glanced to his right and saw DiMarco, Anthony, and Zero at the outside of the track, pumping their fists and hollering. He was running at nearly a full sprint now, and he was two yards clear of the rest. Maybe he could steal this race. Maybe he could out-kick the kickers.

The bell sounded and Manny caught the shout

of the timer: 1:41. He was alone out in front, but he could feel the track shaking behind him. The speedsters were in pursuit. That 30-second last lap Serrano had imagined just might come true after all.

His arms and legs were aching, but that didn't matter at all. Every breath was labored. He moved out slightly from the rail, wanting to make those chasing him work even harder by forcing them to the second lane. He could hear them coming. He could almost feel their breaths.

Down the backstretch, still in the lead. The spectators were all standing now, all urging on their favorites. Manny wouldn't look back. All of his focus was ahead of him.

He raced into the last turn and there was Serrano, his arms swinging as high as his chin as he pumped and churned and pulled even. Manny kept pace. He knew at least two others were less than a step behind him.

Onto the homestretch, that finish line seeming so close he could touch it. Serrano glided past, about to claim the victory. Bertone was right there, his shoulder bumping Manny's. Who else was coming? It didn't matter.

Manny made a final surge and stayed even with Bertone for a few strides, then suddenly pulled ahead. Manny was so close to Serrano that he could have grabbed his jersey, but not close enough to get by. They reached the finish line. Manny was second. He'd nearly done it. He'd nearly won the title.

His first thoughts were confused as he gulped for air. How should he feel? He'd come so close, but he'd lost. Should he be elated or frustrated or both?

His second thoughts were better, as his teammates, his family, and his coach descended on him. Dad grabbed him and pulled him close, and Coach Alvaro rubbed his head.

"Awesome job," Calvin said. "2:14!"

"*Gutsy* race, Manny," said Sherry.

Anthony smacked him on the shoulder. "You took it to 'em."

Serrano came over and they shook hands firmly, then hugged. "It doesn't end here," Serrano whispered. He pointed at the Olympic flag waving high above the track. "We'll be seeing each other, Manuel. We'll be pushing each other to the limit."

Manny grinned. Serrano was right. He'd had a great season, but this was only the start. There were lots of fast races to come.

He looked around the arena. The spectators were on their feet again as older runners raced around the track, locked in a scorching battle for the lead. All around him, sprinters were warming up for the 200-meter races. Coaches were yelling encouragement. A high jumper was soaring over the bar.

Manny had no trouble sorting out his thoughts just then, no trouble identifying his emotions.

He was proud. He was satisfied. He was joyful.

And above all, Manny was a runner.

* * *

READ AN EXCERPT FROM
DOUBLE FAKE
WINNING SEASON #4!

The teams battled frantically as the second half wound down. Calvin had one hard shot knocked down by the goalie, and Danielle came ever-so-close to sneaking one past Zero. But much of the action took place near the center of the soccer field, with constant changes of possession and furious defensive efforts.

Two minutes were left when *Bauer Electric* made a charge down the field, with Johnny and Jessie doing most of the footwork. Calvin stayed between Jessie and the goal, determined that she wouldn't get off a clear shot.

Stop them here, Calvin thought. *We've got time for one big push down the other end.*

Danielle had the ball at the upper corner of the goal box, with Peter right on her. Danielle pivoted and crossed the ball to her sister, who took it at the top of the box, glaring at Calvin.

Jessie feinted left, then moved the ball to the right with the outside of her foot—the same move she'd faked Calvin out with at the preseason clinic. Calvin saw it coming and darted to that side, moving aggressively toward the ball.

And quicker than a bullet—much too quickly for Calvin to react—Jessie stepped on the ball to stop it, rolled it back to her left, and raced straight toward the goal. Calvin stumbled forward. Jessie booted the ball into the net. *Bauer Electric* led, 2–1.

Calvin regained his balance and stared at the sky in frustration. He felt a sharp jab in his bicep. "Sssssssss," said Danielle as she poked him with a finger. "You got burnt so bad you're steaming."

* * *

RICH WALLACE

was a high school and college athlete and then a sportswriter before he began writing novels. He is the author of many critically acclaimed sports-themed novels, including *Wrestling Sturbridge*, *Shots on Goal*, and *Restless: A Ghost's Story*. Wallace lives with his wife and teenage sons in Honesdale, Pennsylvania.